Fashion

by Helen Orme

Trailblazers
Fashion
by Helen Orme
Educational consultant: Helen Bird

Illustrated by Cathy Brett

Published by Ransom Publishing Ltd.
51 Southgate Street, Winchester, Hampshire SO23 9EH
www.ransom.co.uk

ISBN   978 184167 650 0

First published in 2008

Copyright © 2008 Ransom Publishing Ltd.

2

Fashion

Contents

Fashion

Get the facts

What is fashion?

We think that fashion is all about **designer clothes** and that it is something **very new**. But people have been making, buying and wearing fashion items **for thousands of years**.

People began to wear clothes about 50,000 years ago. They decorated their clothes with bones and shells made into beads.

The ancient Egyptians lived in a hot country. Only the richest people wore much clothing. They loved jewellery and make-up. Rich people shaved their heads and wore wigs.

6

The 20th Century

After **World War 2**, everything changed. Until the 1950s teenagers had dressed like their parents, but now they had their own money and they wanted their own fashions.

This is how smart women dressed ...

But teenagers would rather wear this!

The Teddy Boy fashion was the start of teenage fashion. Since the 1960s, teenage fashions have been very important.

The **Teddy Boy** look.

Mods, Rockers, Hippies and Goths

In the mid 1960s many teenagers were either **Mods** or **Rockers**.

The **Mods** wore designer suits and Parka jackets. They rode Vespa or Lambretta **scooters**, covered with mascots. They listened to music by bands like **The Who**.

Rockers wore **black leather jackets**, denim jeans and black leather boots. They liked speed and rode motorbikes. Rockers listened **Rock and Roll** music by people like **Elvis Presley**.

The late 1960s was the time of the **Hippies**. Hippies wore long flowing clothes, big woolly coats and kaftans. They all had long hair.

Are you a Chav or a Goth?

Goths wear black!

Goths like black jeans, leather coats, pointy-toed boots, black T-shirts and dark shades.

Many Goths dye their hair black or bleached blond. Red, white and silver hair is popular too.

Goths go for white foundation and powder with black, red and purple eyeliners and dark lipsticks. The boys wear make-up too.

Goths love jewellery with crucifixes, skulls and bats.

Chavs usually wear designer labels, especially their favourite, 'Burberry'.

The girls wear very short skirts, large hoop earrings and stiletto heeled shoes. The boys wear hoodies or baseball caps and white trainers.

To be a Chav you need to wear a lot of jewellery. The bigger and chunkier the better!

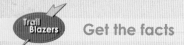

So you want to be a model?

Being a model

There are three main modelling jobs:

Show models

who work for designers. They show the finished clothes to customers.

Photographic models

who display clothes at fashion shows and exhibitions.

Fashion house models

who work in a studio or on location. Some of the top models work for fashion magazines, but most photographic models work for mail order catalogues, advertisements, newspapers and posters.

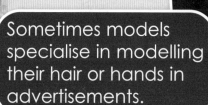

Sometimes models specialise in modelling their hair or hands in advertisements.

What you need to know about modelling

To be a model you need:

 a good figure and complexion

 to be interested in fashion trends, clothes, hair and make-up

 to be at least five feet eight inches (1.72 m) tall, if you are female. Most top models are taller.

BEWARE!

There is a lot of competition. It can be hard to find work.

A lot of modelling work is freelance – if you don't work, you don't earn money.

It is really hard work! Models may have to work out of doors in rain or snow.

They often have to work very long days.

There are not many permanent jobs.

Other jobs in fashion

Do you make your own clothes? Then maybe you could work as a **fashion designer**.

To be a designer you need to be artistic and to be good at matching colours and textures.

Some designers work for the TV or film industry. They design the costumes that actors wear.

Maybe you could be a **beauty consultant**.

Beauty consultants help their customers to choose the right 'look' for their lifestyle and to make the most of the way they look.

Many beauty consultants work in big stores. They might give their customers a make-over.

How about a hat?

Hat designers begin with rough drawings of their designs. Then they decide on the type of fabric and trimming to use.

Fashion Photography is nearly as glamorous as being a model. It can be a very well-paid job.

Fashion photographers take pictures of models wearing the latest clothes and accessories. Their photographs are used in advertisements and catalogues.

The best fashion photographers may travel to exciting places with the models.

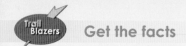
Famous designers

Mary Quant was one of the best-known designers of the 1960s. She made clothes with very short skirts and invented the name **mini-skirt**.

Vivienne Westwood and **Malcolm McLaren** were important designers in the 1980s. They led the punk-rock style, with spiky hair, ripped clothes and lots of tartan.

Zandra Rhodes liked holes, uneven hems and safety pins.

In 1992, **Versace** used safety pins for Liz Hurley's dress. She has been a fashion icon ever since.

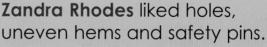

21st Century fashion

We are lucky because modern fashion lets us have a **lot of choice** about what we wear.

> **Colour** is important. Every season different colours come into fashion — and other colours go out of fashion. But remember — **black never goes out of fashion!**

If you look closely at modern fashions, you will see that lots of clothes are very like designs we have seen before. Great fashion is often about wearing **old styles** in **new ways**.

The worst fashions ever?

And you thought modern fashion was extreme!

During the **seventeenth and eighteenth century**, people wore wigs, and the men often wore make-up.

In **Victorian times**, women wore dresses with skirts so wide they could hardly get through the door. They needed a cage to hold the skirts in place.

Before designers invented the cage, women had to wear as many as 6 petticoats, which could weigh up to 7 kilograms.

In the 1960s, women combed their hair into beehive styles. They had to spray the hair until it was almost solid. People used to tell stories about insects living in these hairstyles and boring into women's brains!

Modern extremes

The worst thing about modern fashion is that models think they must be ultra thin. They go on very silly diets which can have tragic results.

A fashion model called Ana Carolina Reston lived on a diet of apples and tomatoes. She died from kidney failure on the eve of a photographic shoot. She was only 21. She weighed only six stone when she died.

Another model, Luisel Ramos, 22, had a heart attack caused by living on a diet of lettuce leaves and fizzy drinks.

1

Fashion
Shoot

Chapter 1:
Fed up

Sam was fed up. Kath was going on again. It didn't matter what he said, she still kept on about it. Kath wanted to be a fashion model.

She was always buying new clothes. She dragged Sam to the shops every weekend. She wouldn't go without him. She said he was really good at choosing things for her.

Sam wouldn't have minded, but they kept bumping in to his mates!

Then he was in real trouble for the rest of the week. Even though Gary, Billy and Joe knew he was only doing it for Kath, they still teased him.

"Who wants to be a model then?"

"Does my bum look big in this?"

No wonder he was fed up!

Chapter 2:
Sam's birthday present

Great! Kath was going shopping again. But she was going with her mates this time.

Just as well. The Rovers were playing at home. There was no way he and the guys were going to miss the match.

His mates arrived nice and early.

"What's that?" asked Joe.

"My new camera," said Sam. "Birthday present. It's really good. I've got all the software too, so I can make great prints."

It was a great match. Rovers won 3 – 2. Best of all, they were close to the action and Sam got some amazing shots.

He spent most of the evening working on them, and printed out the best.

"You should send these to the Echo," said his dad. "They might print them in the paper."

Chapter 3:
A terrible job

Next day Sam went round to Kath's. He took his camera and the pictures he'd taken.

"Oh, football," she said. "Still, they're not bad."

What she really wanted to talk about was a leaflet she'd picked up in the shops.

"Look," she said. "It's a competition. The store wants models. This could be my big break."

"But modelling's a terrible job," said Sam. "Models have to starve all the time."

"I'm not fat!" said Kath.

"Never said you were," sighed Sam. "But I like you as you are."

Kath read the leaflet to Sam.

"They want photos of me. You took great photos of the football match. Now you can do some of me."

Chapter 4:
Come to the store!

They spent all the next week taking photos. Sam moaned, but it wasn't too bad. He was getting well into this photography thing.

Kath got out all her best clothes. She copied the best ideas from her magazines.

Sam took loads of photos. He even studied the magazine pictures.

He got Kath to stand in different ways, just like in the pictures.

He made her stand in bright lights and in shadows.

Kath sorted out the best photos and took them to the store.

She waited for ages. Then the letter came.

"We were really interested in your entry. Please come to the store."

Kath was so excited.

"I'm going to be a famous model!"

Sam went to the store with her.

"I'm afraid we can't use you," they said when they saw her. "You're too short. Models need to be very tall."

Kath was very upset.

"Who took your photographs?" they asked.

"I did," said Sam.

"We can use you," they said. "Your photos were amazing. Do you fancy working in the fashion world?"

Fashion word check

accessories

beauty consultant

Chav

competition

complexion

decorated

designer

extreme

Egyptians

freelance

glamorous

Goth

Hippie

jewellery

lifestyle

location

make-up

mini-skirt

Mod

petticoat

photographer

Punk

Rocker

scooter

studio

style

Teddy Boy

trimmings.